This special edition was printed for Kohl's Department Stores, Inc.
(for distribution on behalf of Kohl's Cares, LLC, its wholly owned
subsidiary) by Chronicle Books LLC.

Library of Congress Cataloging-in-Publication available under
original ISBN 978-0-8118-6690-3.

ISBN 978-1-4521-8178-3

KOHL'S
Style Number: 81783
Factory Number: 131076
Production date: 5/2019
Printed in China

Design by Amelia May Mack and Kayla Ferriera.
Typeset in Creighton.
The illustrations in this book were rendered in mixed media.

10 9 8 7 6 5 4 3 2 1

Chronicle Books LLC
680 Second Street, San Francisco, California 94107

Chronicle Books—we see things differently.
Become part of our community at www.chroniclekids.com.

FOR MICHELLE —A.R.

FOR LEAH, ALEK, AND KYLE —D.S.

CARNIVORES

WRITTEN BY
AARON REYNOLDS

ILLUSTRATED BY
DAN SANTAT

chronicle books·san francisco

THE LION IS KNOWN THROUGHOUT THE ANIMAL KINGDOM AS THE "KING OF BEASTS."

THE GREAT WHITE SHARK IS THE MOST FEARED PREDATOR IN THE OCEANS.

AND THE TIMBER WOLF'S HOWL STRIKES TERROR INTO THE HEARTS OF FUZZY WOODLAND CREATURES EVERYWHERE.

But even **SAVAGE CARNIVORES** get their feelings hurt.

The lion tries to ignore it when the gazelles whisper behind his back. He pretends not to see the zebras looking down their noses at him. The wildebeests call him "bad kitty" just because he's eaten half the neighborhood.

It hurts. It really does.

The great white shark . . . he gets such a bad rap. All those shark movies don't help. Everyone talks about his "feeding frenzies." But he's simply a fast eater.

Nobody understands.

And the timber wolf *almost* never eats little girls. That "Little Red Riding Hood" story is very misleading. The bunny rabbits always say, "Quit sneaking up on me!" But he's not sneaking. He's merely a very quiet walker. With vicious fangs. And scary eyes.

He can't help it.

So it was just a matter of time before the lion, the great white shark, and the timber wolf started hanging out. Because even carnivores need to share their feelings.

At their first get-together, the timber wolf came up with an idea that might solve everything:

"WHEN IN DOUBT, HUG IT OUT."

"We'll go **VEGETARIAN!**"

The lion tried to enjoy his salad . . . but leaves and bark kept getting stuck in his razor-sharp teeth.

The great white shark ate nothing but seaweed for a whole day . . . but it left a horrible kelpy aftertaste in his mouth.

And the timber wolf tried his hardest to eat only berries . . . but every single berry bush seemed to have a bunny inside.

They realized that becoming vegetarians was a silly idea in the first place.

At first, the lion's antelope disguise worked out terrific. Everyone treated him so nicely. But when the other antelopes smelled his zebra breath, it was all over.

The great white shark blended right in with the dolphins.

Nobody suspected him of being bloodthirsty at all . . . until all the dolphins disappeared.

And the timber wolf kept drooling on all the other bunnies.

The disguise idea was a dud. Which was *very* frustrating.
Which made them all hungrier than ever.

As a last resort, the lion invited the oldest and wisest carnivore he knew to come speak to the group. The great horned owl was happy to be included.

"What should we do?" asked the lion.

"Everyone is mean to us," said the great white shark.

"I never know what to say," said the timber wolf.

29 DAYS
WITHOUT
MEAT

The owl smiled. "It used to hurt my feelings, too.
But now I remind myself . . . I'm not bad. I'm a carnivore.
Eating meat is just what I do."

"I'M *NOT* BAD," whispered the lion.

"I'M A CARNIVORE," confessed the great white shark.

"EATING MEAT IS JUST WHAT I DO!" declared the timber wolf.

The wise old owl was **BRILLIANT!**

It turned out he was also **DELICIOUS**.

These days, things are different.
The lion doesn't dread going to the watering hole anymore.

When the zebras give him nasty looks, he smiles his friendliest smile . . . and eats them.

The great white shark feels much better about gobbling up everybody in sight. He knows that he's a husky fish with a healthy appetite.

When the timber wolf gets the munchies, he doesn't think twice about grabbing a handful of bunnies.

They have really negative attitudes anyway.

After all . . . they're not bad.
THEY'RE CARNIVORES.

Eating meat is just what they do.

THE
CARNIVORE
FOOD PYRAMID

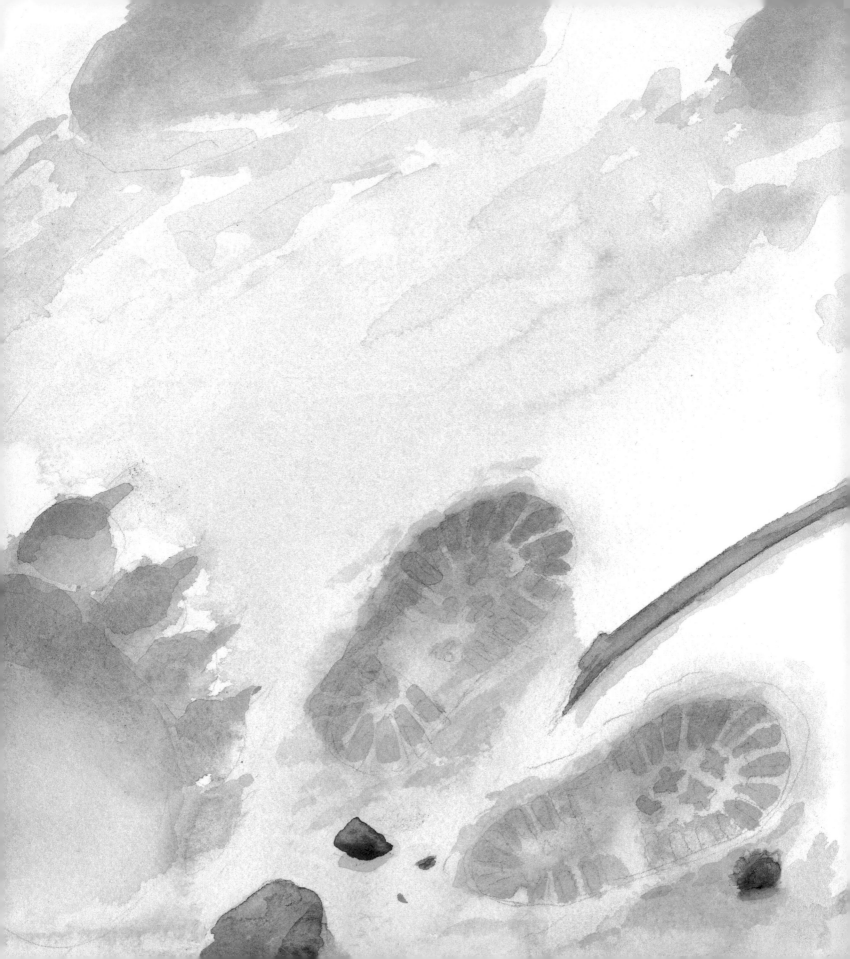

The BEAR REPORT

HOMEWORK

Since we are learning about the Arctic this week, please find three facts about polar bears that you would like to share with the class.

1. _____

2. _____

3. _____

Thyra Heder

Abrams Books for Young Readers
New York

HOMEWORK

Since we are learning about the Arctic this week, please find three facts about polar bears that you would like to share with the class.

1. They are big

2. They eat things

3. They are mean

You are a HUGE bear!
In my HOUSE!

I'm actually short for my age!

My name is Olafur.

I'm Sophie.

Would you like to see
where I live, Sophie?

Um, no thanks.
I've seen pictures.

It's better in person.

There is NOTHING here!

I have a lot to
show you.

Are you hungry?

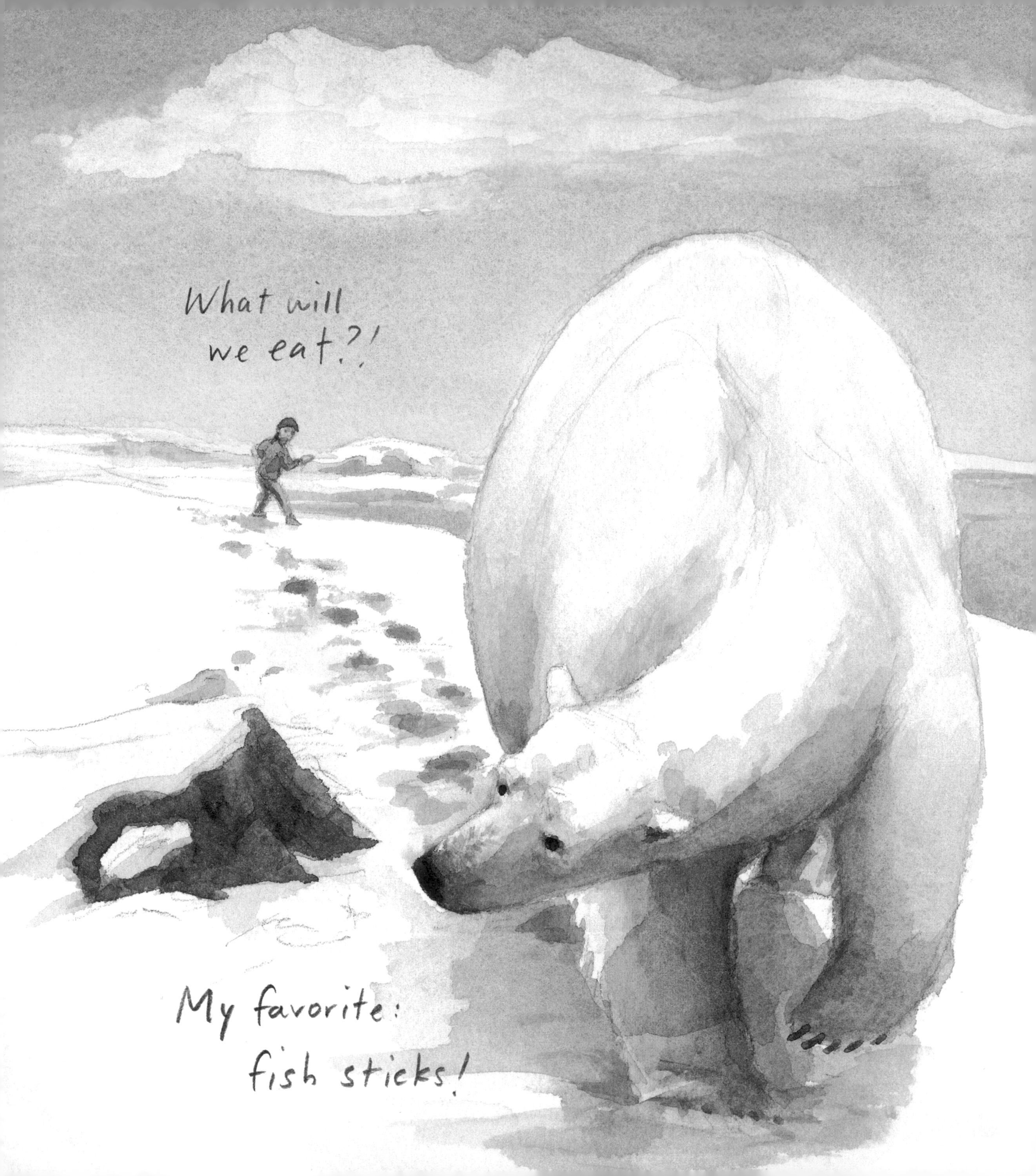
What will we eat?!
My favorite: fish sticks!

What else is
under here?

Seals...
foxes...
snow rabbits.

But they
avoid me.

There's more.

I feel tiny!

Shh!
A buff-breasted
Sandpiper.

This is my glacier
mouse. It's
a rock covered
in moss.

Sometimes I dream I'm a goose.

But a goose can't do

THIS!

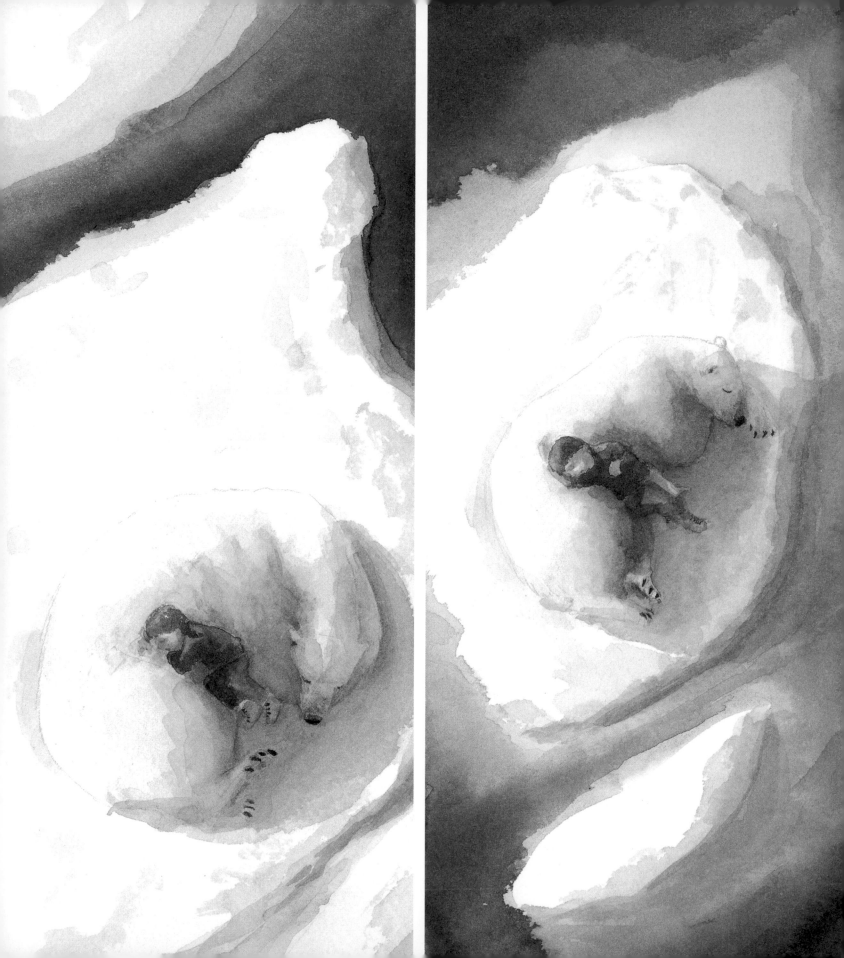

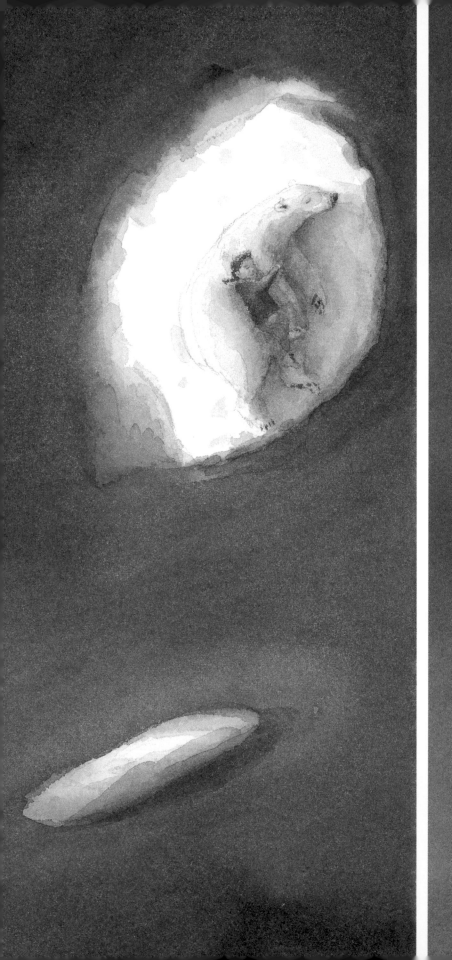

Quick, Sophie,
Wake up.
We have to swim
to shore.

You CAN swim this far, right, Olafur?

I hope so.

But there's nothing else we can do.

That was FANTASTIC, Sophie.
When did you learn to speak whale?

Today!

It's getting dark!

Perfect.
I've got one last
favorite thing to
show you.

I'm going to tell everyone about you, Olafur.

I'm going to tell everyone about you, Sophie.

Author's Note

On a trip to Iceland in May 2014, I went on a guided hike of the Sólheimajökull Glacier. Our guide, Snorri, pointed out where we should not fall: "Death, death," he'd say. Then he'd point to a chasm only slightly less treacherous than the rest: "Serious injury. If you're going to trip, fall in there." As we walked cautiously in our crampons, Snorri talked, and as he talked, we started to learn. I threw rocks in moulins, peered into crevasses, heard rivers gushing below my feet, held mossy rocks that really did look like mice, drank water from ancient ice floes, and scuttled under spiked formations. What at first had felt like nothing but ice now seemed to have a personality, a heartbeat.

I am indebted to the work of photographer Florian Schulz and his book *To the Arctic* (Mountaineer Books, 2011), which I pored over for visual references. In it, he writes, "What I know from my experience, and what I hope to share with those who may think of the Arctic as a nothingness, is that not seeing these creatures does not mean that they are not there, or that they do not need the land."

The illustrations in this book were made with watercolor and ink on paper.

Library of Congress Cataloging-in-Publication Data
Heder, Thyra, author, illustrator.
The bear report / by Thyra Heder.
pages cm
Summary: Sophie is uninterested in writing a research report on polar bears until a polar bear named Olafur swoops her away to the Arctic, where she learns all about the bear's habits and habitat, from glacier mice to Northern Lights.
ISBN 978-1-4197-0783-4
[1. Polar bear—Fiction. 2. Bears—Fiction. 3. Zoology—Arctic regions. 4. Arctic regions—Fiction.] I. Title.
PZ7.H3557Be 2015
[E]—dc23
2014038684

Printed and bound in China
10 9 8 7 6 5 4 3 2 1

Abrams Books for Young Readers are available at special discounts when purchased in quantity for premiums and promotions as well as fundraising or educational use. Special editions can also be created to specification. For details, contact specialsales@abramsbooks.com or the address below.

ABRAMS
THE ART OF BOOKS SINCE 1949

115 West 18th Street
New York, NY 10011
www.abramsbooks.com

MIX
Paper from
responsible sources
FSC® C020056

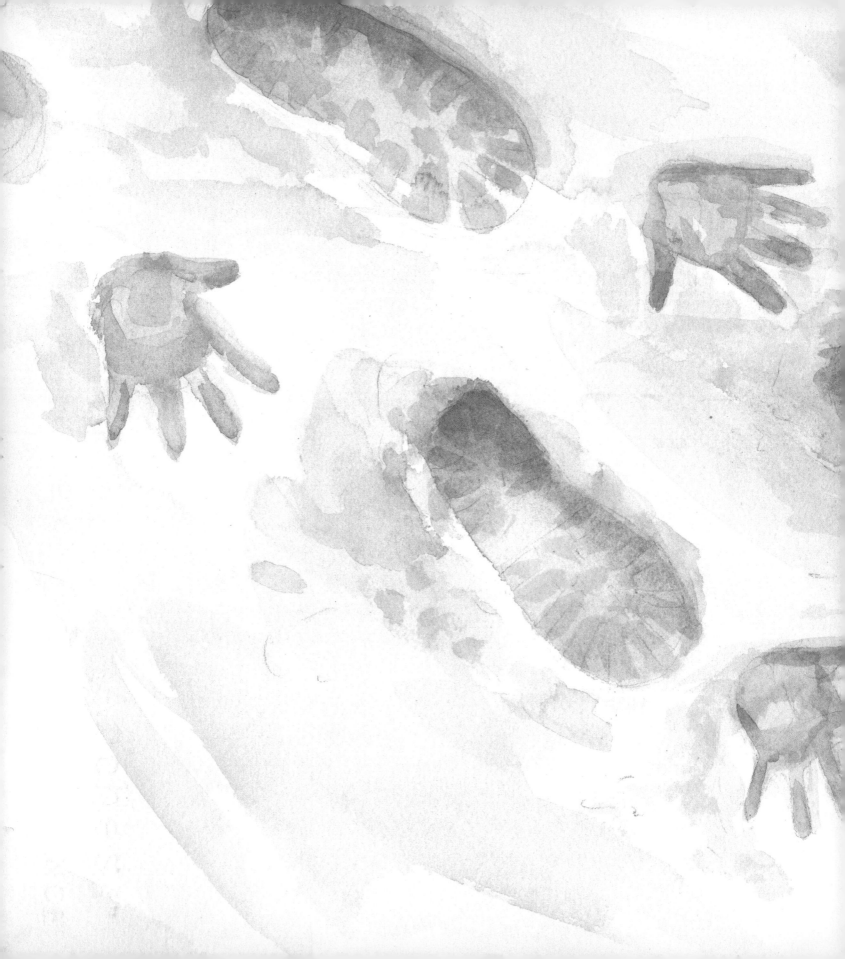